# THE LEAF MEN

and

## THE BRAVE GOOD BUGS

# william joyce

A LAURA GERINGER BOOK
*An Imprint of HarperCollinsPublishers*

There once was an old, old woman who loved her garden. Though her skin was wrinkled with age, it was as soft as the petals of her favorite roses.

"When I was a child," she told the children, "the garden was a miraculous place, and anything could happen on a beautiful moonlit night."

She looked at them sadly. "But that was so long ago, I can hardly remember."

One day the treasured rosebush grew sickly and so did the old woman.

She stayed in bed, and the flowers grew dry from thirst. They began to shrivel and die. The children were sad and uncertain.

So were the insects of the garden.

The crickets serenaded the old lady. The fireflies wished her well.

But she would not wake. Her dreams were fitful and filled with things from long ago. She grew weaker and weaker.

The garden was in peril.

"You must call upon the Leaf Men,"
said the mysterious Long-Lost Toy.
"Only they can save things now."

"The Leaf Men are not real," sneered
the Spider Queen. Her ant goblins croaked
and laughed, but the Toy ignored them.

To call the Leaf Men," the Toy explained, "one must climb the highest tree, and as the full moon touches the topmost branch, sing out low and sure, 'Leaf Men . . . Leaf Men . . . we are in need.'"

The insects had never known the Toy to speak. For countless days and nights he lay silently in the grass, lost and forgotten. His mystery had never been solved.

The insects had heard stories of the Leaf Men, but they were unsure. It would be a perilous journey to the top of the tree. No garden bug had ever gone so high.

A tiny troop of doodle bugs assembled.

"We of the Doodle Bug Guild will face what must be faced!" their leader proclaimed.

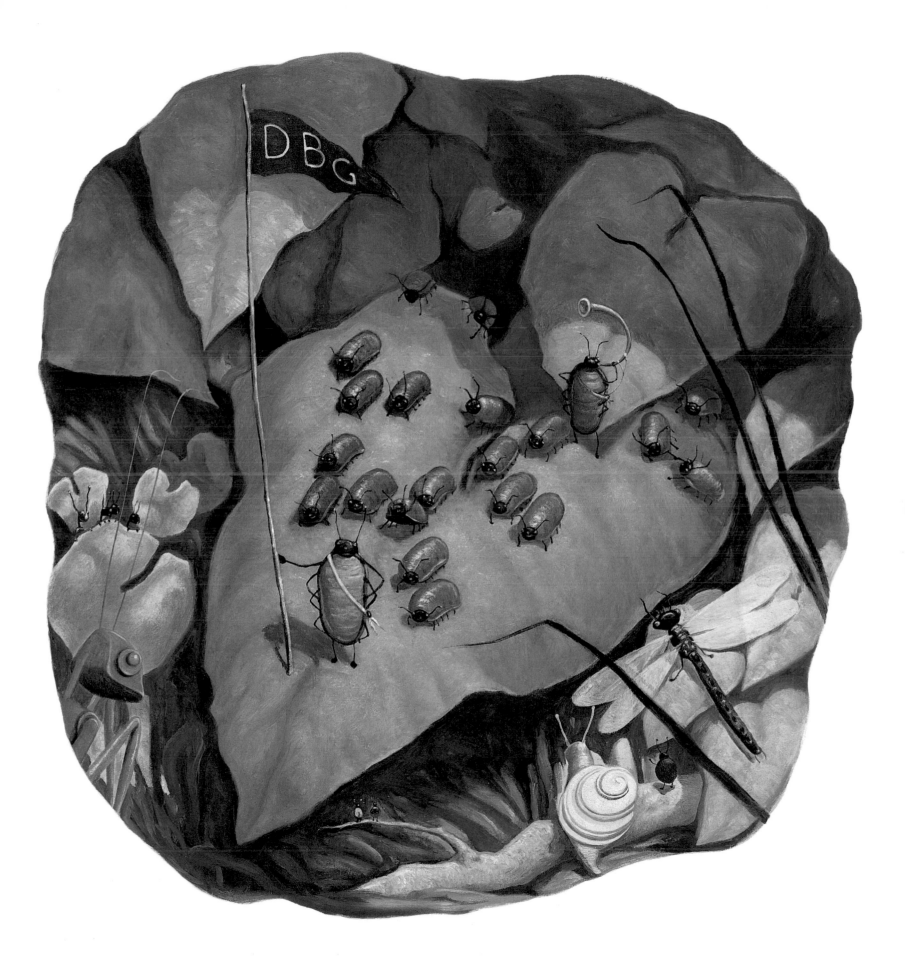

The Spider Queen laughed at them, but the doodle bug leader stopped her short. "Tiny of body but brave of heart, we will finish what we start!" he said proudly.

This angered the spider.

The Long-Lost Toy smiled. He'd never liked the Spider Queen.

It was windy as the doodle bugs began their climb. A storm was brewing.

The other insects wished them well but wondered if they could make it.

Night fell as they journeyed ever upward. The moon appeared through swiftly moving clouds.

The wind grew stronger, but the doodle bugs were not afraid.

They chugged along, racing with the moon to the top of the tree—a tiny train of brave good bugs.

They were almost to the treetop when lightning flashed! The sky rumbled! Giant raindrops smashed down!

And *then* the Spider Queen appeared.

The doodle bugs rolled up tight to save themselves, but doodle bug bowling was just what the Spider Queen hungered for.

"No spider snacks are we!" shouted the doodle bug leader. He tickled a goblin and got away.

"Leaf Men!" he called out. "Leaf Men, we are in need!"

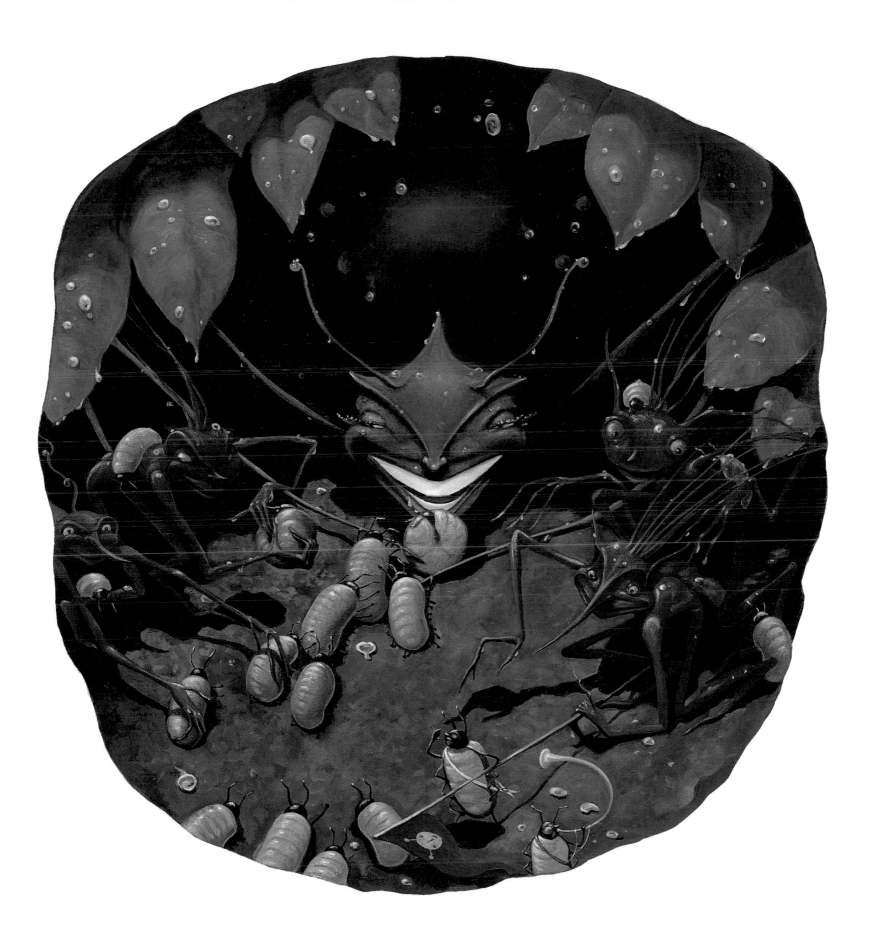

The storm stilled. The air grew quiet. And there stood the Leaf Men, ready to lend a hand!

From branch to branch the battle raged. With arrows made of thistle the Leaf Men shot the spider through the heart. Her goblins fled in horror.

The valiant Leaf Men then whisked the doodle bugs earthward by way of Luna Moth.

The Leaf Men were gardeners of a grand and elfin sort. They sewed leaves back on, turned brown stalks green, and made the rosebush bloom like new.

"Tiny of body but brave of heart, we always finish what we start!" sang the doodle bugs as they helped. But when the gardening chores were done, the Leaf Men grew quiet. . . .

"The Spider Queen at last is dead," they told the Long-Lost Toy, "and only *you* can save things now."

At dawn the old woman finally woke. Her eyes lit up.

"My little metal man!" she whispered. "You've been lost for so long!" She had not seen him since she was a little girl. "I'd almost forgotten you," she sighed. She smelled the rose in his tiny hand. Then she saw footprints on the windowsill and smiled.

Soon the old lady was back in the garden. "I remember now," she said. "My father gave me the metal man to watch over me at night. My mother planted the rosebush to bring me comfort. I remember they told me that the Leaf Men watch over the garden and make sure everything's all right."

Is that true?" asked the boy.

She smiled and hugged them both. "Things may come and things may go," she said. "But never forget—the garden is a miraculous place, and anything can happen on a beautiful moonlit night."

The Leaf Men and the Brave Good Bugs

Copyright © 1996 by William Joyce

Manufactured in China. All rights reserved.

Library of Congress catalog card number 95-40644

First Edition, 1996

in
memory
of
John